Zanna's Gift

Zanna's Gift

A LIFE IN CHRISTMASES

Scott Richards

A Tom Doherty Associates Book
New York

ZANNA'S GIFT: A LIFE IN CHRISTMASES

Copyright © 2004 by Scott Richards

This book is printed on acid-free paper.

Edited by Beth Meacham

Book design by Jane Adele Regina

A Forge Book
Published by Tom Doherty Associates, LLC
175 Fifth Avenue
New York, NY 10010

www.tor.com

Forge® is a registered trademark of Tom Doherty Associates, LLC.

Library of Congress Cataloging-in-Publication Data

Richards, Scott, 1949-
    Zanna's gift : a life in Christmases / by Scott Richards.—
1st hardcover ed.
        p.   cm.
    ISBN 0-765-31237-9
    EAN 97-0765-31237-2
    1. Girls—Fictin. 2. Women artists—Fiction.
    3. Brothers—Death—Fiction. I. Title

    PS3618.I3445Z36 2004
    813'.54—dc22

                                        2004050629

First Edition: November 2004

Printed in the United States of America

0   9   8   7   6   5   4   3   2   1

To Dad and Mom,

for a house full of art
and glorious Christmases.

Spring and Fall

Margaret, are you grieving
Over Goldengrove unleaving?
Leaves, like the things of man, you
With your fresh thoughts care for, can you?
Ah! as the heart grows older
It will come to such sights colder
By and by, nor spare a sigh
Though worlds of wanwood leafmeal lie;
And yet you will weep and know why.
Now no matter, child, the name:
Sorrow's springs are the same.
Nor mouth had, no nor mind, expressed
What heart heard of, ghost guessed:
It is the blight man was born for,
It is Margaret you mourn for.

—Gerard Manley Hopkins

Zanna's Gift

1

There are many ways to lose a child, and none of them is merciful. But like all unbearable things it can be borne, and in the weeks before Christmas 1938, the Pullmans were learning how.

Ernie, their oldest boy, had turned fifteen in August and was in his next to last year of high school. There would be little money to send him to college, but he was smart and studied hard. He hoped for a scholarship.

But he didn't count on it. He

didn't count on anything. That was why he also worked at Virgil's Furnace.

Ernie had started with Virg as a boy, looking over the man's shoulder while he worked on eking some more life out of the Pullmans' old coal-burner.

"Can't be saved," said Virg, and then told them the bad news about what a new one would cost.

Ernie spoke up before his parents could say a thing. "What's the cost if I go to work for you?"

Virg looked the boy up and down—which wasn't far, he was only ten at the time, and not big for his age. Ernie had watched closely during the attempted repair. He'd made himself useful, fetching this and holding that. And his questions showed that he understood what Virg was doing.

So Virg looked at Mr. and Mrs. Pullman and said, "I'll take him on, but I can't say how much it'll take off the price till I see what his work is worth."

"That's fair," said Ernie, again before his

parents could respond. "I'll make sure the discount is good and big."

Ernie learned so fast and worked so hard that in the end, his parents paid exactly what their furnace had cost Virg. And Virg kept Ernie on, helping with repairs and installations and helping with the books, too, until, at the age of fifteen, he was the unofficial junior manager.

The other two furnacemen and the coal truck driver might have resented this, but Ernie had such a respectful way of talking that it never felt as though he was giving orders to men twice or three times his age.

Half the money he earned, he handed over to his father. The other half went into the bank, for college.

Mr. Pullman was proud of his oldest son, saying little about it, of course, because a man didn't gush about such things, it would only embarrass the boy.

Mrs. Pullman, on the other hand, looked with suspicion on the teenage girls who had a way of routing their walk to school past the

Pullman house, on Lily Street. She knew perfectly well what a prize catch her boy would be, and knew there wasn't a girl alive who was worthy of him.

Ernie's two younger brothers, Davy and Bug (short for Beadle, a name which even Mrs. Pullman, whose mother's maiden name it was, now realized had been a mistake), worshiped Ernie, but from afar. Ernie had always looked out for them, but never fought with them or bullied them or, as they got older, played with them. He was too busy, and they were too in awe of him, for roughhousing or rivalry.

But when Suzanna was born in spring of '34, Ernie took her to his heart. Only to hold fussing baby Zanna would he interrupt his homework, and she seemed to quiet most quickly in his arms, looking up into her brother's face as he cooed to her in a voice that Bug declared was sickening enough to make a grown man puke.

She sat on his lap while he studied, until she was old enough to crumple the pages or seize the pencil, and then he bought crayons and paper for her out of his own money and encouraged her to draw.

Zanna was no scribbler—instead of bold strokes, she made tiny, meticulous curlicues and filled-in dots, working for long stretches of time to fill just one corner of a piece of paper.

Then she would slide it over to Ernie, who would look up from his books and papers, examine the drawing carefully, and then look steadily into her eyes.

"I know it's a child," he might say, "but I don't know who."

"'S not a child," Zanna would say—or sounds to that effect. "It's a dog."

"But it's a very young dog." He pointed to another part of the drawing. "And I don't appreciate the way that dog is nipping at me while I'm trying to get a new furnace hauled into the Petersons' cellar."

And she would giggle at the fantasies he spun around her incomprehensible art.

Gradually, though, her art became comprehensible to him, and it wasn't long before his guesses were usually right.

Nobody else understood how he did it.

One night, after four-year-old Zanna was in bed and asleep, Mrs. Pullman held up her night's work and asked Ernie, "How in the world did you find a car on this paper?"

He pointed to a spiral near the bottom. "That's how she makes wheels."

"But there's only one."

"She only draws one in detail. Those dots are the other three tires."

"She puts all four tires on a car? You can only see two at a time."

"She's short, Mom. She sees all four."

"OK, but where's the rest of the car?"

"That's the steering wheel. That's Dad driving the car."

"They're just twisty little spirals."

"But that one has a nose, so it's a person, and that one's on a stick, so it's the steering wheel. Who would be driving except Dad?"

"Why doesn't she draw the whole car?"

"She has an eye for the round parts," said Ernie. "It's like the whole world is a big connect-the-dots, and all she bothers to draw are the dots."

"What Ernie's saying," said twelve-year-old Davy, "is that Zanna's crazy, but he's crazy the same way."

"Yep," said Ernie.

Zanna never heard that conversation, but she knew that Ernie was the only one who understood her drawings, and so it was only natural that all her drawings were for him. She didn't bother showing them to anyone else. *He* showed them off, explaining them to everybody else, while Zanna beamed in pride.

Zanna knew that drawing was the best thing she did. Her only evidence for this belief was that Ernie understood and praised her pictures. But that was more than enough for her to be convinced she was an artist of extraordinary merit.

2

*E*rnie could have died so many ways. Furnace work was dangerous; there were accidents. When he rode his bike to and from work, he had to share the road with automobile drivers who, as Mr. Pullman often pointed out, were murderers in their hearts.

But there was no accident.

Nor was Ernie ill. Oh, he'd had a cold as the weather started turning nasty in late October, but that was gone except for a sniffle now and then, and a little huskiness in his voice.

There was no warning at all. Ernie went to bed on the first Monday night after Thanksgiving, and did not get up in the morning. His mother noticed at once that he had not gotten up at his usual time, but her thought was, The poor boy, he works so hard, how can I begrudge him one morning of sleeping in just a little? She kept expecting him to rush into the kitchen as she breakfasted the other kids, frantic about being late and demanding to know why she hadn't woken him, and she planned to just smile and pretend not to have noticed the time.

But then it grew late enough that he might not be able to make it to the bus on time, so she left Davy in dubious charge of the kitchen table and went to waken Ernie in his room.

He was lying there peacefully on his side, his body curled like a question mark under the blankets, one leg drawn up, the other extended, the way he always slept. But when she spoke to him he did not stir, and when she shook his shoulder it did not yield.

Was he sick? She felt his forehead for

fever, but it was as cold to her hand as tap wa-
ter in winter.

She knew then that he was gone. She had
dressed both her mother and father for burial;
she knew how a dead body felt under her hand.

It was so impossible, though, that he
could be dead, that she simply walked out of
the room and closed the door behind her and
went back to the kitchen. She interrupted the
inevitable fight between Davy and Bug and
wiped up the pile of congealing oatmeal that
Zanna had made beside her bowl. Calmly,
emotionlessly, she explained that Ernie was ill
and wasn't going to school today, and fended
off Zanna's attempt to go see him. "I don't
want you catching it, Zanna."

Davy and Bug were out the door and on
their way, bundled up against the cold—their
school was in walking distance. Mrs. Pullman
got Zanna some crayons and paper, knowing
that she would concentrate totally on her
drawing for quite some time. Only then did
she call the doctor, keeping her voice low and
her explanations oblique, so that Zanna would
hear little and understand less.

"You must come look at my son, Ernie," she told Dr. Wood. "His forehead is very cold, and he doesn't move."

It took Dr. Wood a moment to register what she was saying.

"My four-year-old is here in the kitchen with me, Doctor," said Mrs. Pullman, "and I hope that when you come, you can handle things quietly for her sake."

"I'll be right there," said Dr. Wood.

It took him only ten minutes. He found Mrs. Pullman very calm, except for the handkerchief she was wringing and twisting around her fingers. Wordlessly she led him to Ernie's room and closed the door behind them.

When the doctor rolled him over, Ernie's arms and legs stiffly held their positions. It was grotesque, and the doctor could not bear to have Mrs. Pullman remember her son in such a state, so he rolled the boy back. He went through the motions of looking for signs of life, but rigor mortis was obvious.

"He must have passed away in his sleep almost as soon as he went to bed last night," said the doctor quietly.

Mrs. Pullman nodded.

"There was nothing you could have done," said the doctor. "Did he complain of being sick?"

She shook her head.

"It could have been his heart," said the doctor. "Sometimes the heart is weaker than anyone knows."

"His heart," said Mrs. Pullman almost angrily, "was *very* strong." Then she let out a single great sob and slumped against the wall, burying her face in her handkerchief.

"Would you like me to call your husband?" asked the doctor.

She nodded.

"And is there a neighbor I can ask to come over and sit with Suzanna?"

Mrs. Pullman nodded and pointed toward the south. Dr. Wood went there first, explained briefly to Mrs. Higham, who immediately scooped up her own two-year-old daughter and hurried over.

"Come and play at my house, will you, Zanna?" said Mrs. Higham.

"I'm busy," said Zanna.

"Your mother really needs you to come to my house so she can take care of Ernie. I'm baking cookies."

But Zanna had no interest in cookies. She bent over her drawing.

"You can finish your drawing at my kitchen table." When Zanna didn't answer, Mrs. Higham put a hand on her shoulder. "Sweetheart, you really must come."

Zanna gathered up her crayons and paper and followed Mrs. Higham through the autumn cold. Only then did the doctor dial the number for "Dad's Work" beside the telephone on the small table in the parlor.

Mr. Pullman came home at once, and bore the news as calmly as if he had been expecting it. He took his weeping wife into his arms and held her, nodding as the doctor suggested that he could have Ernie's body taken to the hospital to try to determine the cause of death.

Mr. Pullman shook his head.

"Won't you always wonder why he passed away?" said Dr. Wood.

Mr. Pullman said, "I don't want you cutting into him."

Mrs. Pullman sobbed again and Mr. Pullman helped her slump into a chair.

"Mr. and Mrs. Pullman," said the doctor, "I'm sorry to be blunt, but the undertaker will also open the body in preparation for burial. Please let me try to find out why such a strong and fine young man was taken from us."

They seemed not to be listening. Until the doctor added, "What if it's a hereditary condition that might affect the other children?"

So it was an ambulance, not a hearse, that came to the Pullman house, and the men who carried Ernie's body from the house wore white, not black.

It turned out not to have been Ernie's heart at all. As the doctor explained it to the parents, something in his brain broke open and killed him instantly. "It could not have been predicted," he said. "It could not have been prevented. It was just his time."

"No it wasn't," said Mr. Pullman quietly.

"Hush, dear," said Mrs. Pullman, but her voice was tender and her hand gentle as she rested it upon her husband's hand.

"It was not his time," said Mr. Pullman, but his voice was soft, his insistence more of a murmur to himself than an argument.

"No, I agree," said Dr. Wood. "It was *not* his time. A boy like that should have had a long life."

"He had greatness in him, Doctor," said Mrs. Pullman.

And as they left his office, Dr. Wood saw that now it was Mrs. Pullman who comforted her husband, who seemed to have aged ten years in the day since his firstborn son had died.

3

The Pullmans had told the children separately, because the explanation that the boys could accept would not have been right for Zanna, being only four, and so devoted to her brother. The boys were told the simple truth, with some comforting words about the resurrection and heaven, where someone as good as Ernie was bound to go.

But Zanna was given the story of a journey to a faraway place, from which Ernie would not be coming home.

"Yes he will," said Zanna.

"I'm afraid not, darling," said Mother.

"He'll be home for Christmas," said Zanna firmly.

Father put his hand on Mother's shoulder. It was enough for now.

Mrs. Higham tended Zanna during the funeral. Zanna never saw her brother in the casket. Nor did she see her mother cling weeping to Ernie's hand, or her father bend over and kiss his son's lips before lowering the lid of the coffin with his own hand. It would not be until years later, when her brother Davy told her what he remembered of it, that she acquired her imagined memories of that parting.

At the time, though, she only knew that Ernie did not come home, and her parents looked so sorrowful that she felt the need to comfort them.

"Ernie will write to us," she said. "You'll see. You don't have to miss him so much."

But this did not seem to comfort them after all, and young as she was, Zanna realized that there was something they were not telling her.

Her mother cried so easily these days that Zanna went to her father with her question, one night after supper, when she was supposed to be getting ready for bed.

"Ernie's dead, isn't he?" she asked.

Father looked at her for a long moment, and then nodded.

"Can I give Heavenly Father a message for him in my prayers tonight?" asked Zanna.

"Whenever you want," said Father.

"Heavenly Father won't forget to give him my message, will he? Sometime you forget to give a message."

"Heavenly Father doesn't forget anything," said Father.

But Zanna knew what Father's voice sounded like when he was angry, but trying to hide it.

"Don't be angry at Ernie," said Zanna. "I bet he didn't mean to die."

"I'm not angry at Ernie," said Father. "I'm just sad."

"So am I," said Zanna, and then, as if to prove it, she burst into tears and buried her face in her father's lap as he stroked her hair and her back and murmured words of comfort and love.

But her tears ended as quickly as they began. She stood up and dried her eyes on her sleeve and said, "I have to get ready for bed now so I can say my prayers."

Father wanted to explain to her that she didn't have to wait till she was in her nightgown to say a prayer, but she was out of the room too quickly for him to form the words.

So instead he got up to warn his wife that Zanna knew, and that her prayers would be hard to listen to tonight. Father and Mother held hands as they listened to Zanna's message for her brother. It was simple enough. She loved him. She missed him. She wished he wasn't dead. She hoped he wouldn't miss her too much in heaven.

Zanna didn't cry again until she was in bed. Her mother offered to stay by her bed, but Zanna shook her head, and her parents left the room as she cried herself to sleep.

Children are resilient, and their emotions come and go quickly, as their minds turn from thought to thought. Zanna was as cheerful as ever the next day, and the day after, and when she talked about Ernie sometimes it sounded as though she had forgotten he was dead, and sometimes it sounded as if he had died many years ago, and she was completely used to the idea. Her parents were grateful that Zanna was taking it so well—better than her brothers—and also admitted to each other that they envied her the peace in her heart.

4

$\mathcal{C}$hristmas would come to the Pullmans with the cold logic of the calendar, and the parents decided that the best consolation for the children was to make the season as normal as possible.

So only a week after the funeral, Father came home with a Christmas tree tall enough to brush the ceiling before he cut down the top sprig to make room for the star. He strung the lights, and he and Mother and the children spent the whole evening hanging up all their decorations.

By sheer force of will, the parents did not succumb to memories of how Ernie had strung the lights and hung the star for the past three years. In fact, they acted their part so well that the evening was full of laughter; even Davy, who had been so solemn since his brother died, laughed and teased Bug. And Bug, for his part, was sweet with his little sister and helped her hang ornaments on low branches, and this year did not try to rehang all the ones that she had placed.

After the children were in bed, the parents sat in front of the festive tree and held hands, and Mr. Pullman said, "We still have all these children, and they're good ones, too."

Mrs. Pullman nodded. "I know."

"It's right to make things normal for them," said Mr. Pullman.

"Yes, it is."

Then they wept and held each other, thinking of the boy who should have been there, and who had been taken from them so untimely.

A few days later, Davy came home from school late. Mother began to scold him, but he stood up rather defiantly and said, "Don't you want to know where I was first?"

"Well, where were you?"

"I was at Virgil's Furnace," he said. "Virg says I can start there as an assistant and learn the work by helping, the way Ernie did. And I promised that I'd work every bit as hard as Ernie did, even though I'm not as smart and probably won't learn as quick."

"You're a very smart boy," said Mother.

"Not as smart as Ernie," Davy insisted. "Nobody is."

"Well I'm proud of you," said Mother. "And I know Ernie will be. But you really do have to work hard, and stick to it."

Father was also proud when he got home from work, but he had another worry. He took Davy out onto the back porch and put his arm on his son's shoulder and said, "Davy, you know that you don't have to try to take Ernie's place."

"If I don't, who will?"

"Nobody will," said Father. "You have a place of your own, and it's every bit as important and good as Ernie's, and we love you every bit as much."

"So you don't want me to work for Virg?"

"I want you to do whatever you think you should, and I want you to do the best job you can," said Father. "But do it because that's what you want, and not because it's what Ernie did."

"All right," said Davy.

But Father knew that he had made little headway, and it would be some time before Davy could find his way out of his brother's shadow.

Well, there *was* time, wasn't there? Davy would have many years to work his way through his life.

Or else he wouldn't. He might die in his sleep one night, and then what did it matter whether he was in his brother's shadow or not? What did anything matter?

Father shuddered at the thought, and felt the slight shoulder of the boy under his hand, and said to himself firmly: This one is alive, and so something *does* matter. I did not die with Ernie, and neither did my duty to my family.

There's nothing in life that you can be

sure of keeping—he had known that even be-fore Ernie died. This was not the first loss or grief in the Pullmans' lives, just the first one that the children shared in. You could spend your life missing what you had lost and fearing to lose what you had, or you could take such joy as God gave you and rejoice in the children who were still with you. Mr. Pullman already knew what choice he would make.

A few days later, it was Bug who asked the most disturbing question of all. "What are we going to do with all the money Ernie saved up for college?"

Because Father wasn't home, and Mother was utterly unprepared for the question, she answered with a question of her own. "Why do you ask?"

"I just thought maybe we could use some of it to buy presents for each other the way Ernie would have."

"Ernie would never have used that money to buy presents," said Mother. "It was saved for a purpose."

"But he won't be going to college now," said Bug.

That was too much for Mother. She didn't cry, but she did press her lips together in the effort *not* to cry, and shook her head, and Bug knew the conversation was over and left the room with a murmur of "Sorry, Mom."

Still, the question of Ernie's savings was an important one. Mr. Pullman, being an accountant, had helped several families deal with the taxes and expenses involved with a death and inheritance. As he explained to his wife when she told him about Bug's question, "Ernie died without a will, and so by law all his possessions belong to his next of kin, which would be his parents."

"But it's still his savings," said Mrs. Pullman. "How would he want us to use it, that's the question."

"He never touched his savings for Christmas presents."

"But he won't be going to college now," said Mrs. Pullman, firmly. "So what would he do with the money now that *that* purpose is gone?"

In the end, they decided to divide his savings into three parts. As they explained to the children at a family council around the kitchen table, "This money was meant to pay for college, and that's what it will do—it's the start of your college savings, all three of you."

"What's college?" asked Zanna.

"It's a school for big people," said Bug.

"And after you go to college, they have to pay you more money," said Davy.

"Ernie never touched his college savings," said Father, "and neither will you. You can add to it by what you earn as you get older. And it will gather interest."

Whereupon Bug asked what "interest" was, and the meeting quickly degenerated as Father tried to explain the entire banking system to children who soon grew desperate to get away.

How much of this Zanna understood was impossible to guess, but a few days later it became clear that she had understood at least this much: They had to decide what to do about things that had belonged to Ernie.

It was only a week before Christmas, and Mother was in the kitchen baking date bread to take to the neighbors for Christmas.

Zanna came in carrying a paper with lots of coloring on it.

"Mommy," she said. "What about my present for Ernie?"

"Well, darling, I'm afraid you'll need to give it to someone else who might use it."

It was only after Zanna had trotted back out of the kitchen that Mrs. Pullman realized that Zanna hadn't bought a gift for Ernie. He had died before any Christmas shopping had taken place. So what did she mean? Did she think they could give Ernie Christmas gifts after all? What was going through that little four-year-old mind?

It became clearer that night when she found Zanna crying in her bed.

"What's wrong, darling?" asked Mother.

"I can't give Ernie's present to anybody else."

"Why not, darling?"

"Because nobody else likes my drawings."

So it was a gift she had *made* for him. Of course. But then . . . when had she made it? Was it possible that she was already thinking of a Christmas gift for him before he died?

That she had already drawn him a picture?

"Ernie saw all your pictures, darling, and he loved them all. It's not your fault that he left us before he got to see this one."

"But this one is the best one ever."

"May I see it?"

Zanna slid out from under the blankets and opened her bottom drawer and took out a piece of paper.

Now that Mother looked at it, she could see that it really had been a labor of love. Instead of consisting of a lot of tiny drawings in the corners of the paper, there was only a single picture in the middle, bigger than anything Mother had seen Zanna draw.

"It really is special," said Mother. "What is it?"

Zanna started to cry. "Nobody ever knows what my pictures are, except Ernie."

And in that moment Mrs. Pullman realized that in Zanna's world, the loss of Ernie had been just as devastating as in her own. She pulled her daughter into her arms.

"Oh, my little darling, my sweet girl, I'm so sorry. Ernie loved your drawings, and I bet

41

Heavenly Father will let him see what you drew."

"But Ernie won't ever be able to tell me that he loves it."

"No, he won't," said Mother. "Not until you get very old and Heavenly Father takes you home."

Zanna raised her red and tear-soaked face to look at her mother. "I can never make a drawing for him again!" she wailed.

"Darling," soothed her mother. "Darling, that's not true. It's just not true. You can make *all* your drawings for him. Your whole life, every drawing, can be for him. Don't you think he'll be watching you from heaven? Don't you think that he can see?"

Again Zanna's face, so full of misery, looked up into Mother's. "Can he?"

"I don't know," said Mother honestly. "But Heavenly Father loves you, and loves him, and don't you think that he would let him see your pictures?"

Zanna thought about that and shook her head. "I want to give him the picture."

"I know, darling."

"He really wants this picture! He asked me for it!"

"I know, but you can't."

"He asked me for it *special*. He said for me to do it for him for Christmas. And then he died before I was finished! It's not fair. I was working on it every day. I couldn't do it any faster."

There was nothing more that Mother could say. She just held her daughter close and shed her own tears into Zanna's hair until her daughter finally fell asleep and Mother lifted her into bed.

5

Zanna's grief over the gift she couldn't give did not fade, as Mother had thought it would. Instead, the child moped all day. Even as she helped with the baking and laundry-folding and other tasks that usually were times of chatter and play between mother and daughter, she wore a face of sorrow. It hurt her mother's heart to see how Zanna suffered, but what could she do?

As Christmas grew closer and Zanna did not forget, Mrs. Pullman talked about it several times with her husband. There was talk of getting a dog; then they remembered that any puppy they brought home now might well die while Zanna was in her early teens, and even if it lived till she went to college, the last thing she needed was to be set up to lose another loved one.

"It's out of our hands," Mr. Pullman finally said, and that night when they prayed together, Mrs. Pullman asked the Lord to give comfort to their little girl this Christmas, since it wasn't in their power, needing comfort so badly themselves.

When Zanna came bounding into the kitchen the next morning with a big smile on her face, Mrs. Pullman's first thought was, Since when does God answer prayers that fast? And her second thought was, Why is God so attentive all of a sudden, when he could have avoided all of this by just letting Ernie stay alive?

"I'm glad to see you smiling today," she said.

Zanna nodded. "I saw Ernie last night."

Mother stiffened a little. Maybe God had

gone a little far. "Was it a nice dream?" she said.

"Yes," said Zanna, and Mother relaxed. As long as Zanna knew it was a dream.

"He didn't say anything," said Zanna. "In my dream I tried to tell him about the picture. But I couldn't make my mouth work."

"You were asleep, darling," said Mother.

"No I wasn't. I could see me right there, holding his hand, only I couldn't make me do anything. I couldn't even make me show him my picture."

"You saw yourself?"

"I was standing right by him, and I was looking at me just like he was. And then he turned to the me that was standing by him and picked her up and I kept wishing that he had picked up the me that was really me instead of the me in the dream, because I couldn't feel him pick me up and I bet *she* could."

What a strange dream, thought Mother. To have yourself in it twice.

And then she thought of another explanation.

She thought of the other grave, beside Ernie's. The one that none of the children, not even Ernie, had known about, because there had been no reason to grieve them on an occasion so happy as the birth of their only sister.

She almost burst out with the idea right then. But no, it might be too much for Zanna, at her age. So she kept it to herself. "I'm glad you had that dream, darling, and I'm glad it made you happy."

And in a part of her mind that she wasn't proud of, she thought, While God is handing out comfort, wouldn't it be nice if I could see my boy just one more time, even if it's only in a dream, and even if it's someone else's hand he's holding, and someone else he hugs?

But she swallowed that thought, too, for Zanna's sake, and kept on about the work of the morning.

It wasn't till afternoon, when Zanna was down for her nap, that she phoned her husband at work and told him about Zanna's dream.

"I don't know," he said. "Either it was just

a dream, or it was something more, but how can we tell?"

"The little girl in the dream. Don't you think it could have been Dianna?"

There was a catch in her husband's breath. "Well, then it would have to be something real, wouldn't it? And that's an answer to prayer, and we should be glad of it."

"That's all?"

"What more can we do?"

"I just wondered if we made a mistake not telling Zanna about her sister."

"We probably did," said Mr. Pullman. "But is this the time?"

"If God's going to show her . . . I mean, maybe it *was* a message to us. That we should tell her about something that God has already shown her in a dream."

"Or maybe she was just dreaming about Ernie and her together, and she thought of the girl as someone separate from herself because Ernie's out of reach now."

"So I shouldn't do anything about it?"

"I don't know," said Mr. Pullman.

They finished the conversation, but a few minutes later he called her back.

"I'm coming home," he said.

"What for?"

"Because it's Christmas Eve," he said, "and it's insane to stay here working when nobody expects me to and work isn't taking my mind off things anyway."

She waited a moment, because the tone in his voice sounded as though there was another item on the list of reasons why he was coming home.

There was.

"I want to take them out to see Dianna's grave. I think it's the right thing to do, whether it was God who sent us a message or just a dream."

"Whatever you think."

"What do *you* think?"

"I was wishing we could do it. I was thinking of waking her up and taking her, and trying to get back before the boys got home from school."

"Then it really *is* the right thing to do, if both of us wanted to."

"Only I want to tell her first," said Mrs. Pullman. "Just her."

Mr. Pullman thought for a few moments.

"I'm coming home now. I'll be there when the boys come home. You take her and explain it."

"Oh, I couldn't do it without you!"

"You're right. She should hear about it before her brothers. It was her dream, and Dianna was her twin."

6

Zanna was sleepy, and dozed on the trolley. But it was only a nap, and the bell soon woke her up. She looked eagerly out the window until Mother told her where they were going. Then she became quite still and listened.

Because Zanna hadn't been there at the funeral, and they had avoided burdening her with too much knowledge for her four-year-old mind to absorb, she hadn't understood about burials and why we treat the empty bodies of our loved ones with such care and put them in the earth, even though their souls were in heaven.

"So Ernie isn't really there," Mother said. "But we go there to remember him."

"I can remember him at home, too."

For a moment Mother wondered if Zanna was saying that she didn't want to go, but Zanna was kneeling on the seat looking out the window with such interest that Mother realized that she had simply been reminding Mother that she didn't have to go to a cemetery to remember.

They walked through the chilly air and over the browning grass to the freshly turf-covered grave that had no headstone yet.

"We don't have a marker for Ernie's grave yet," said Mother. "They're still making it. The stonecarver is."

"What if they forget where he's buried while he's making it?"

"They won't forget," said Mother. "The grave is still new. And besides, there's another marker that will help them remember."

She led Zanna to the stone at the head of

the grave just to the right of Ernie's. It had been obscured from view by some of Ernie's flowers during the funeral, so people wouldn't ask questions about it; Ernie's funeral should be about Ernie, not interrupted by difficult explanations.

The inscription on the marker said:

DIANNA PULLMAN
17 April 1934

**An angel God would
not be parted from**

Mother read it to Zanna.

"She has our same last name," said Zanna. "And that's my birthday."

"She's your sister, Zanna," said Mother. "She was in my tummy with you. She was born the same day as you, but something went wrong for her inside my tummy. You were born first, but when she came out, she only lived a few hours. I got to hold her for a little while, and so did your father, and she lay beside you for a little while before she died."

"I don't remember," said Zanna.

"I know," said Mother. "You were just a newborn baby. Nobody remembers things that happen on the day they were born."

"I didn't know I had a sister."

"We never told you. We never told your brothers, either. They were so happy to have you come home. We didn't want them to be sad to think of the sister who *didn't* come, when there you were, to have all their love."

"Does Daddy know you had another little girl?"

"Yes, darling. I told you—he held her before she died. We loved her but then she was gone, and we still had you, so we were sad and happy at the same time. And we've been happy every day of your life to have you with us."

Zanna thought about this for a while. "Do you miss her?"

"Oh, yes," said Mother.

"But you never talk about her."

"Your father and I do, though. We talk about her sometimes. Every now and then, Daddy says to me, Too bad Zanna has to live in a house full of boys. If only she had her sister with her. She wouldn't be so lonely."

"I'm not lonely," said Zanna.

"I know. But we can't help wishing you had your sister with you."

Zanna looked up at her mother. "Do you ever wish you had her instead of me?"

"No!" cried Mother. "Never, darling. You are the light of our life, don't you know that? We wish there were two, but since we have only the one, we love that one with all our heart and we're glad every day that we have you. Don't you know that?"

Zanna nodded, but then pulled away from her mother to look again at the gravestone. She reached out and touched the name.

"Dianna," said Zanna. "That rhymes with Suzanna."

"Because you were twins," said Mother.

"What's that?"

"You looked alike. You looked just exactly alike, and if she had lived, you would look so much alike today that if you dressed the same, nobody but me and your father would be able to tell which of you was which."

"So how do you know I'm really Zanna?"

"Because they put little ribbons on you in

the hospital just as soon as you were born. You got the pink ribbon, and she got the yellow one. We named the pink-ribbon baby Suzanna and the yellow-ribbon baby Dianna."

"Can I see the ribbons?"

"Yes," said Mother. "We keep both the ribbons in a box at home. Along with a picture of you and your sister together." She did not tell her that the picture was taken just after Dianna had died. Since Zanna was sleeping when the picture was taken, they both looked the same.

"Can I come back when you have Ernie's stone, so I can see his name?"

"I promise. We'll come back many times in years to come."

"But we never came before," said Zanna. "And she's been here my whole life."

"Your father and I came," said Mother. "And now you'll come sometimes, too."

Zanna put her arms around the headstone and leaned her face down on the cold granite.

"Darling," said Mother, reaching out as if to draw her away.

"Now I know," said Zanna.

"Know what, darling?" asked Mother.

"Why I didn't feel Ernie hug me in the dream."

"Do you?"

"It was Dianna. He even said so."

"I thought he didn't say anything."

"He called her Dianna when he picked her up and hugged her. I thought he said Zanna and I just heard him wrong. But he said Dianna."

Mother didn't know what to say, because she couldn't tell from Zanna's face or voice how she felt about this.

"It's only fair," said Zanna. "It's her turn. I had him for all this long time and she didn't have anybody, not even her mommy and daddy."

Mother started to cry then. She'd been doing so well up to that moment, but she realized now that God *had* sent her comfort after all, in Zanna's dream. Ernie and Dianna were together. It had to be true, it had to be from God, because Zanna hadn't even known that her twin existed. And even though it brought a new flood of tears, Mrs. Pullman was comforted to think that her lost son and her lost daughter had found each other.

It was in the trolley on the way home that Zanna remembered her Christmas gift for Ernie.

"She'll draw all his pictures for him now," she said.

"I guess that's so," said Mother. "It might very well be so."

Zanna leaned her head against the window and closed her eyes. "But now there's nobody I can give the picture to, and it's my very best. I'll never do another one as good as that."

"You can give it to me and Daddy," said Mother.

Zanna made a face. "You don't even know what it *is*."

"That's true," said Mother. "But you could tell me."

"It's not the same," she said, "when you have to tell."

"But it's the best we can do."

Zanna turned around on the seat and leaned closer to Mother. "It's a picture of me and Ernie. He's reading to me. He was reading *The Bobbsey Twins of Lakeport* to me."

Then her eyes grew wide. "Mommy, do you think he knew *I* was a twin, just like the Bobbsey Twins?"

"He knows *now*, doesn't he?"

"Don't tell Daddy about the picture," said Zanna.

"Why not?"

"Because maybe he'll guess my picture. Without me telling him."

"I don't think so, darling," said Mother. "We're not good at it like Ernie was."

"I know," said Zanna. "But maybe."

Then Zanna had a thought and glared at her mother. "Don't you tell him and then let him *pretend* that he figured it out!"

"I won't," said Mother, who had been planning to do exactly that.

"That would be a *lie*!" said Zanna, who had only recently learned that lying was bad.

"I won't tell him," said Mother. "But you mustn't be disappointed if he doesn't guess right."

Zanna fell silent till they reached their trolley stop, which came quite soon. They had chosen a cemetery that wasn't far away.

Her brothers were already home from school, and she ran straight to them and announced at the top of her lungs that she had a twin sister who looked just like her only she died the day she was born and now Ernie was with her and she saw them in a dream and now Ernie was reading the Bobbsey Twins to her and looking at *her* pictures and he always knew just what they were, and probably nobody ever knew what her pictures were until Ernie came, and that's a long time to make pictures that nobody can see.

Davy and Bug were skeptical until Mother assured them that yes, indeed, there was a twin named Dianna, who had died the day she was born.

It was clear that the boys didn't like the fact that they had never been told, and they also didn't like it that Zanna had been told first and even shown the grave, and not them. Davy even complained about it to them after supper, when Bug and Zanna were out of the room and Davy was helping clear up the dishes.

"We had to tell her first, Davy," said Father. "It was her twin sister. She had to be told before anyone else."

He wasn't buying it, and was sullen for several minutes afterward. But Mr. Pullman winked at his wife and took the dishtowel from her. "We men will finish this up." It never took Father long to jolly Davy out of a mood, so Mother willingly left them to their work.

She went into the parlor and found Bug and Zanna sitting close together on the couch. *The Bobbsey Twins of Lakeport* was open on Bug's lap, and he was laboriously reading to his sister. Zanna was leaning her head on his shoulder as he read. Mrs. Pullman stepped silently back out of the room and leaned against the front door for a long minute, breathing deeply and thanking God for sending her such good children and blessing their home with comfort in a hard season.

7

$\mathcal{I}$t was a good Christmas morning, all things considered. In years past, the parents had always been woken by Davy and Bug laughing and yelling as they tried to get past Ernie, who was the guardian of the door to the parlor. This year, though, Mr. Pullman awoke to see that the clock already said seven-thirty, and there wasn't a sound from the children.

He shook his wife awake. "They let us sleep in," he said.

"They're probably already in

the parlor unwrapping everything," she said.

But they weren't. They were in the kitchen, and Davy had made cheese sandwiches for Bug and Zanna. "I don't know how to make oatmeal," he said, "and I don't know how to break an egg without making a mess."

Cheese sandwiches were an excellent Christmas breakfast, Mother said. The thicker and chunkier the slices, the better, said Father.

And as the parents joined in the unconventional breakfast—adding some sliced banana and glasses of juice to the mix, so they'd be fortified against the candy they expected Santa had put in the children's stockings—Father finally had to ask, "Well, how's the haul this year?"

The kids looked at him blankly.

"How did we do? Did Santa spill his sack? Or is it just coal for us all this Christmas?"

Davy looked at him like he was insane. "How should *we* know?"

"You haven't been in the parlor?"

"That would spoil Christmas," explained Bug patiently.

When breakfast was finished, Father got

out his camera and waited in the parlor for the children to come in one by one, snapping their faces as they saw the tree and the presents. Just like normal. Except that there was one fewer picture.

Everyone thought about Ernie, but no one said anything. The children didn't mention him because they knew it might make their mother cry and their father sad. The parents didn't speak of him because they couldn't have done it without breaking down and crying, and they didn't want to spoil Christmas for their surviving children.

So Ernie's name remained unspoken, and the whole ceremony of unwrapping presents one by one was unusually solemn, until the very end.

"Well, that's all the presents," said Father.

"No it's not," said Zanna.

"Oh?" said Father. "I don't see any others."

"It's in my room," said Zanna.

She ran out and came back a few moments later, carrying the picture she had made for Ernie.

Mother was afraid she meant to give it to

Father as a test, and that it would spoil Christmas for her if he failed to guess what it was: She had kept her promise not to tell.

Still, there was always a chance he might guess right. So she held her breath.

Father, on the other hand, was afraid that Zanna expected them to give the picture to Ernie somehow. He didn't think he could handle going out to the cemetery today and putting his daughter's drawing on his son's grave.

But if that's what she required of him, he'd do it.

Instead, she stood in front of all of them and held up the picture. "This is a picture of Ernie reading the Bobbsey Twins to me. I made it for Ernie for a Christmas present and it's the best picture I ever made."

"It's beautiful," said Father.

"It doesn't look like anything," said Davy.

"*I'm* reading you the Bobbsey Twins now," said Bug.

"I know," said Zanna impatiently—though which brother she was answering was unknowable. Probably both.

"So it's the last present," said Zanna. "But

I can't give it to him. So here's what. I'm going to save it for him."

Davy made a face and looked away. Bug answered her a little testily. "He's not coming back."

"I know," she said, as if it were the stupidest thing she'd ever heard. "But someday I'm going to go see *him*, and I'm saving it for him till then."

"You can't take pictures with you when you die," said Davy.

"I'm not stupid," said Zanna, "I'm four. By the time I'm old like Mommy I won't even remember what my picture looks like if I don't keep looking at it."

This seemed to make sense to her brothers, and despite the tears in his eyes, Father had to smirk a little at Mother because Zanna had called her "old."

But Zanna was as good as her word. She saved the picture she had made for Ernie, and the next Christmas she brought it out of the bottom of her drawer and had it beside her as she opened all her gifts.

And the Christmas after that, when she

was six. Mother had thought for sure she would forget; and Father had forgotten about the picture himself until Zanna brought it in.

The next year, when Zanna was seven, Davy's present for her was a picture frame, just the right size to hold Zanna's picture for Ernie. He carefully put it in behind the matte and reattached the thin wood backing.

"That way it won't get all beat up in your drawer," he said. "It'll stay nice."

Davy was now the age Ernie had been when he died, and Father and Mother agreed, when they spoke together later of his gift to Zanna, that he was every bit as fine a boy as they could have hoped.

"If growing up in Ernie's shadow causes a boy to be as sweet as Davy is, then his shadow is a pretty good place to be."

The years passed. The world went to war, and when Davy was eighteen, he enlisted, instead of waiting to be drafted. His mother wanted to make him promise to be careful, but Father wouldn't let her. "He's not going to war to be careful," he told her. "He's going to serve his country. He's going to save the world.

He wants to be brave. He wants to make a difference with his life."

"I know," she said. "But I just . . ."

She didn't have to finish the sentence. Father knew that two of her five children were
buried already, and she did not want to lose
another, lying in a foreign grave like so many
young men in the First World War.

But they were fortunate. By the time Davy
had finished his training, the fighting was over
in Europe, and even as his troopship carried
him across the Pacific to prepare for the inva-
sion of Japan, two atomic bombs were dropped
and the Japanese surrendered. He didn't get to
come home that Christmas—he was on occu-
pation duty—but the family knew he was safe.
Probably having the time of his life.

The Christmas when Zanna was fifteen,
the family was all together again, perhaps for
the last time, because Lucy, the girl Davy had
brought home to meet them, was from California, and he was planning to move out there
and go to school on the GI Bill at a university
near her family's home.

Everybody was so excited at meeting the

girl that Davy was hoping to marry that the present-opening was almost over before Bug turned to Zanna and said, "Zan! Did you forget?"

She looked at him blankly. "Forget what?"

"The picture!"

For a moment, Zanna looked puzzled, and then when she remembered, she looked embarrassed. Not because she had forgotten, though—her quick glance at Lucy made it clear to her mother that she was embarrassed to bring out such a childish picture in front of someone that she wanted to impress.

"Zan, darling," said Mother, "you don't have to if you don't want to."

Then Zanna thought better of her reluctance and said, "I do want to, Mom. But you tell about it while I'm gone, would you?"

Before Zanna could even leave the room, Lucy spoke up. "I wondered if you'd let me see the picture. I wasn't going to ask because it's a private family thing, but Davy told me all about Ernie, and Zanna's present for him, and I was hoping you'd like me well enough to let me see." She put her hand over Davy's. "I know what it's like to love somebody so much you want to keep them with you all your life."

They all fell in love with her at that moment, and when Zanna brought the picture back, Lucy held it and studied it.

"Nobody can ever see anything in it," said Zanna. "I draw a lot better now."

"I know," said Lucy. "Davy already told me which of the paintings on the wall were yours."

"It's me and Ernie," explained Zanna.

"He's reading to you from *The Bobbsey Twins*," said Lucy. "My father read me that book when I was little. It made me wish I were a twin. I wish you could have known your sister."

"It's kind of a silly book," said Zanna, suddenly shy again.

"But it isn't when you're little," said Lucy. "I'll always love it. And now I'll also think of it as a book you shared with your brothers." Lucy glanced at Bug then, so it was plain that Davy had told her that Ernie wasn't the only one who read the book to Zanna.

It occurred to Mrs. Pullman then that Zanna's gift for Ernie had become something important to the whole family. Even though no one but Zanna had ever been able to see Ernie's face in that drawing, that picture held his face for all of them. And when that picture was present in the parlor on each Christmas morning, it was a way for Ernie to be with them, too, in their hearts, in their memories, and still part of their lives. And Davy had shown them a thing she couldn't have hoped for—that he hadn't brought home a girl for them to meet without first making sure that she knew about the children they had lost so many years ago.

The truth was, they all saw Ernie's face in Zanna's picture now. Just not with their eyes.

8

*Z*anna took the picture with her when she married Hal and moved to the coast. Why shouldn't she? It was her picture.

But as their first Christmas together approached, she was shy about bringing out the picture. He had seen her recent artwork, of course—they had met in a figure drawing class, where he sometimes modeled to pay his way through college. She knew that he'd be delighted to see that she had kept a drawing from her childhood.

But he was bound to wonder

why it was so cheaply framed and why it had to come out and sit on the top of a bookshelf on Christmas Day, as if it presided over the gift-giving. She would have to explain.

What if he didn't get it? What if he thought it was something cute, and teased her about it? She fell in love with him partly because he was such a tease—but what if he didn't understand that this wasn't something she could bear to be teased about?

Without meaning to, she was setting him up to be tested. That wouldn't be fair to him, and if he failed the test it would create a barrier between them.

She began to wish she had left the picture home. Mother and Father would have brought the picture out for her, and even though she wouldn't be there, it was the house, the very room where Ernie had celebrated all his Christmases. It belonged *there*, not here in this city of strangers.

And from there it was a short step to realizing that *she* belonged there—at home for Christmas, with her parents. What was she doing here in an apartment, a building, a city where she was the only one who knew that Ernie had even existed?

Hal came into the bedroom and found her crying and at first he quietly kept his distance. Then he sat down beside her and put his arm around her shoulder and said, "Miss your folks?"

She nodded.

"I miss mine too," he said. Then he gently squeezed her shoulder. "You're my folks now, Zanna."

She gave one big sob and threw her arms around him. "You're my folks, too, Hal. Really! I was only missing them because . . ."

When she didn't finish her sentence, he made a stab at it himself. "Because it's Christmas and it doesn't feel right without being home with all the—"

"No, no, it feels *absolutely* right to be here with you."

He accepted that for a few silent moments. Then: "But you *were* crying, and I may be crazy, but they didn't seem like tears of joy to me."

"It wasn't my folks I was missing, really. I

mean, not my parents. Or Davy or Bug—Davy and Lucy and their kids are the only ones going to be there with Mom and Dad anyway, Bug's away, too and . . ." And again, she couldn't think how to even begin.

"So you were missing somebody else."

She was stunned. "How did you know?"

"Because you said it wasn't your folks you were missing. So it had to be somebody else."

"Oh, of course." Her laugh was only the tiniest bit hysterical. "I thought maybe Mom or Dad had told you. Or Bug—he's the big talker, he—"

"Zanna, baby, you never left me alone with any of them long enough to *have* a private conversation."

"Didn't I?"

"I was never quite sure if you were afraid *I'd* say something wrong, or *they* would, but both times we visited them before the wedding and all through the whole wedding weekend itself, you were right there making sure somebody didn't make an idiot of themselves. I just assumed it was me. But now it appears there's something you haven't told me.

So let's have it. I know you don't have a wooden leg and both your eyes are real, so—"

"Please don't tease me about this," she said.

"I don't even know what it is I'm not teasing you about," said Hal.

She pulled the picture out of the box she kept under the bed and gave it to him.

"Is this a new style you're working with, or an old one?"

"I was four years old when I made it. It was a Christmas gift. In 1938. It's a picture of my brother Ernie reading to me."

He studied the picture. She waited for him to make some comment about how he couldn't see any such thing. Instead he said, very softly, "I didn't know you had a brother who died."

"I was halfway through drawing this when he died, and I was so young and understood so little about death that I went ahead and finished it because I thought I could still give it to him somehow, but when I found out I couldn't, I kept it, and Davy bought the frame for me, and that Christmas Bug even finished

79

reading me the book that Ernie was reading, so in a way they're both here in this picture, so it's all my brothers. And in a way, it's my sister, too."

He looked at her with tears in his eyes. "Of course you were afraid to show it to me," he said. "What if I teased you about it?"

"No, I know you'd never do that!"

"Are you kidding?" said Hal. "If you'd just shown me this picture and said it was something you did as a kid, I'd have teased you up one side and down the other, and *then* when you told me what it meant I'd have felt like the lousiest husband they ever invented."

"But you didn't tease me, Hal."

He grazed his fingers across the glass. "This isn't art anymore, Zanna. It's magic. Your family has saved up all kinds of love in here. But what I can't figure out is, how could they bear to let you take it away?"

She shook her head. "That's what I was crying about, really. Because the picture belongs in my parents' house at Christmas. But it also belongs with me. I couldn't stand it if I let it go. It would be like telling Ernie I don't love him anymore. And I *do* still love him. He was the best person in my life. Till you, of course."

Hal kissed the top of her head. "I hope someday to earn that. But remember that Ernie had a whole four years, and I've only known you for just over one year, so it'll take me a while to catch up. It helps a lot that you told me this. And now I know why I got you the gift I got you for Christmas."

He got up and went into the front room. She almost got up to follow him, but before she could decide, he was back, holding the red-wrapped gift he had set there proudly two nights before.

"Open it," he said.

"But Christmas is day after tomorrow."

"Has to be right now. Has to be before the post office closes this evening."

She tore open the wrapping paper and opened the box and there was a complicated looking camera. "I don't know how to use these things."

"Doesn't matter," he said. "I do. The camera isn't so much for you to use it yourself, though I hope you learn how, because it isn't hard. It's because so many times you've said how you wish you could paint something but you just don't have the time even to sketch it. Well, this is a Polaroid Land camera. It doesn't just take the picture, it develops it, too. In about a minute, there it is."

"That must have been expensive."

"Very," said Hal. "I'm sorry, but I had to pawn our firstborn child. It was a fellow named Rumpelstiltskin, I knew you wouldn't mind."

"But this is wonderful. Of course it means you have to go with me when I look for scenes to paint."

"Whenever you ask, if I can get away from work, you know I'll be there. But that's not why I had you open it early."

In a few minutes, they had Zanna's picture of her and Ernie propped up atop a bookshelf, and Hal took three photographs of it. He had obviously studied the instructions in advance, because he knew every step of what seemed to Zanna to be a pretty complicated procedure. All three pictures turned out—a good sepia-toned rendition of the picture, frame and all.

Then they put the photographs into envelopes and sent them by Airmail Special Delivery to Bug in Kansas City and to her parents and Davy back home.

"They might not make it to everybody before Christmas," said Hal. "But they'll know we tried. And next year they'll have them for sure."

At the post office, as she watched Hal slide the two envelopes through the slot, she felt herself almost overwhelmed by relief and love and happiness. "I think I married the most wonderful man who ever lived," said Zanna.

"You just keep thinking that," he said as he hugged her. "Do you know who I married?"

"Just me, I hope," she said.

"I married the kind of girl who can love somebody forever." He kissed her. "I'm that same kind of man."

9

$\mathscr{T}$he Pullmans were an American family and their grown-up children did what Americans were doing in the 1950s: They moved, not from neighborhood to neighborhood or town to town, but from state to state, and Bug even had a stint in Germany working for a company that was trying to redesign its product to appeal to American consumers.

Most Christmases, though, one or another of the kids would come home, so Mr. and Mrs. Pullman were rarely without company during the holidays. And on the mantel, presiding over Christmas, there was always a photograph of Zanna's gift—at first the sepia-toned Polaroid, and later a framed color photograph. Each of the brothers had their own, just like it.

There were also a couple of family reunions, with Davy, Bug, and Zanna bringing all their kids back to the family home—usually in the summer, though, because the house was too small and the parents too old to have so many kids cooped up inside. The cousins all knew each other, and by any standard the family stayed close no matter how farflung their residences were.

The best part about family reunions, Zanna thought, was getting to know her brothers' kids. It was also, unfortunately, the worst part. At first Zanna tried to find, in each child, whatever aspect of them came from a particular parent. Oh, that's how Bug was at that age—but this *other* trait must come from Bug's wife Sylvia.

Only it didn't hold up, not really. Each girl was her own self, each boy found his own way.

You couldn't look at children and hope to see much of their parents beyond their physical appearance, and not always that. They came, as Wordsworth said, "trailing clouds of glory." Along with a few clouds of other things not quite so glorious. The adventure was to find out who they were.

Bug's third child and oldest boy, Todd—not named Ernest because Davy had already taken the name for his first son—*he* was a problem. What was it that made a perfectly normal, healthy boy with parents who doted on him into a such a lying little sneak?

That was a horrible thing to think of him, Zanna knew, but she had never actually heard him say anything that didn't have some kind of lie hidden in it somewhere. Though it hadn't become obvious until her own children were involved and she had to sort out the difference between her own child's version of events and Todd's. The first few times it happened, she had actually taken Todd's word over her own children's. Todd was so convincing, and her kids' versions were so outrageous.

Until the family reunion when she was

coming back from the public restroom at the park where they were having their big family picnic, and she actually saw Todd drop to his knees in a patch of mud. There was no one around him; he just plopped in it and then used his hands to get back up and wiped them on his pants.

Strange boy, that's what Zanna thought. She even mentioned it to Hal and Davy when she joined them by the fire where the hot dogs were being burnt in stripes.

When she went looking for her kids to eat the franks before they were pure ash, she ran across Bug lecturing her two oldest, Patty and Lyle, about how some pranks weren't funny, they were mean.

"What did they do this time?" asked Zanna. "I thought things were going too smoothly."

"Oh, they shoved my Todd down in the mud over there. It's all over his pants."

This was illuminating. She waited for Patty to wail about how she didn't do it, and Lyle to get belligerent. But they just hung their heads in shame. It almost made her be-lieve that they were guilty.

"Did you do it?" asked Zanna.

Lyle just stared at the ground, and Patty's head-shake was almost imperceptible.

"Lyle, Patty, I *know* you didn't do it," said Zanna.

They looked up at her with such surprise and hope in their faces that she was almost ap-palled.

"What are you saying?" said Bug. "Todd doesn't lie."

"Then I'd have him checked out with a shrink, because he's hallucinating," said Zanna. "I came out of the john and saw him, clean pants, standing all by himself at the edge of the mud patch, and then he plunked himself down right on his knees, got up and wiped his hands on his pants. Does that sound like what he looked like when you saw him?"

"But Zan, it doesn't make any sense. Why would he make it up?"

"Bug, that's between you and Todd," said Zanna. "I'm not even interested. I just know that my kids are not going to get blamed for something they didn't do."

"Are you so sure they didn't do it?" demanded Bug.

Zanna just laughed at him. "Bug, before you accuse *me* of lying, maybe you'd better consider the possibility that Todd's got a little tiny streak of aimless malice in him."

"What are you saying about my son?" Bug demanded.

"I'm saying that I love you dearly, Bug, and I trust you to take care of your own children however you choose. But I'm not going to let Todd ruin this reunion for Lyle and Patty by getting them in trouble for something that I know for a fact Todd did all by himself." Then, kids in tow, she headed off toward the food.

"What I want to know," said Zanna, "is why you weren't even bothering to defend yourselves, even when I asked."

"What good would it do?" asked Patty.

"You never believe us," said Lyle.

That's when she remembered *why* she had asked Bug "What did they do this time?"

Every reunion, her two oldest got in trouble—but only now did she make the connection that they got in trouble for something they did *to Todd.*

"This has happened before," said Zanna.

"Last year we told you and told you we didn't push his face in the cake," said Lyle. "He's taller than me anyway, how *could* I? And Patty wasn't even there. But you didn't believe us, and so we didn't get any cake."

"And you made us apologize to him in front of everybody," said Patty.

"That's why we hate coming to reunions. Because he always does stupid stuff and says we did it and nobody believes us."

"I'm so sorry," said Zanna. "I'm just sick about it, just . . . sick. You poor things. But to me it just . . . it made no *sense* for him to . . . I mean, how could I know until I saw it for myself that he just . . . he must have just pushed his *own* face into the cake last year and—"

"Tell us something we don't know," said Lyle snidely.

She couldn't even rebuke him for being snippy with his mother.

"Well, now I know what Todd is like," said Zanna, "I'll believe you. I should have believed you all along. I mean, I'm so stupid. You never do things like that at home. Not to each other, not at school. Why would I think you'd . . . but it was so impossible that he'd be making it up." She shook herself. "*Oh* this could make a person insane. Listen, I was wrong. And I'm sorry. I can't do anything about Todd—"

"You mean Toad," said Patty under her breath.

"Yes, I mean Toad," said Zanna. "That's between his parents and him. But I'll never take his word over yours again."

The two kids glanced at each other.

"Wait a minute," she said. "I saw that look. So let me rephrase. I will never take his word over yours *at first*. But don't take that as permission to do any mean thing to him that you want and I'll stick up for you."

Lyle grinned at her.

Patty was miffed. "I wouldn't and you know it."

"But Lyle was thinking of it, weren't you, Lyle?"

"I was just wondering if somebody was dumb enough to bring another cake this year and leave it lying around."

So that was Todd, whose malicious lying was not some hereditary trait—Bug and Sylvia were so honest they couldn't *conceive* of having a lying child. It was just something he brought with him. Along with the clouds of glory.

But there were other nieces and nephews. Like Bug's oldest daughter, Betty. She was such a tomboy, right from her knack for practically vaulting out of the crib so that you had to stay with her and watch her every second. She could throw a ball harder than most boys— which meant stones and snowballs, too, and with deadly aim. There wasn't a tree whose loftiest branches she hadn't climbed until Grandma yelled herself hoarse about how they had to *get the child down* and *why doesn't somebody do something* and *won't somebody please tell her that she's a girl?*

"Girl schmirl," said Grandpa. "Somebody needs to tell her about gravity."

It wasn't a fall from a tree or fence or roof that ended Betty's daredevil days. It was polio.

Todd was almost five, then, showing no sign of the malice that surfaced later—and Bug's other girl, Cindy, was only seven when they came to live with Zanna and Hal while Bug and Sylvia stayed with Betty around the clock as she struggled for life.

When she finally emerged from the iron lung, she had little use of her legs. It was a milestone when she finally got on her feet. It almost broke Zanna's heart to see her that Christmas, a ten-year-old clunking around the house with two heavy leg braces, and still having to lean on walls and the table to keep from falling over.

But Bug still swung her up into his arms, leg braces and all, and she still knew how to whoop with delight when he did it.

That was almost the most heartbreaking thing about it. A girl who had been so active— polio should have made her glum, surly, even angry, but it didn't.

Oh, there were times.

Zanna remembered coming into the parlor that first Christmas after the iron lung, and seeing Betty standing at the window, looking out at the other kids up to their knees—or higher—in snow. It was such a day as had once been Betty's glory. She should have been up a tree raining snowballs down like the wrath of God on Sodom and Gomorrah.

But she and her leg braces were stuck inside, and Zanna stood in the doorway, her heart breaking for this beautiful child. Breaking twice: in grief for what she had lost, and in joy for how Bug's and Sylvia's prayers had been answered.

For she could see another face—Bug's haggard expression when he brought the little kids to stay with her and Hal. He was facing the death of his own child, as Betty lay struggling just to breathe in a far-off hospital.

"I thought I knew," he told her then, quietly, when Hal was showing the kids where they'd be sleeping. "What it was like for Mom and Dad to lose Ernie. I mean, we lost him too, didn't we?"

Then suddenly his face crumpled and tears burst from his clenched eyes and he clung to her. "Oh, Zan. I pray to God you never know for yourself. It's the worst thing in the world."

But seeing him like that, and thinking of her own Patty and Lyle and baby Colleen, she could imagine. "They hold us hostage," said Zan. "We make these children and we love them so much and the world holds them for ransom and any time it wants to, it gives us the note and demands that we pay."

He pulled away from her then. "Anything. Just so she lives."

She wanted to ask him then, Even crippled? But she knew the answer already—yes, even crippled, just *don't* take her.

Then Bug got control of himself before his two younger kids came crashing back into the room. It wouldn't do for them to catch their papa crying, would it?

So as she stood at that window, several years later, and watched Betty watching the other children outside in the snow, she could just imagine what yearning the girl must be feeling—and how bittersweet it was for her parents to see her like this, still alive, but now held by such heavy chains to the earth. Now she knew more about gravity than anyone else.

Yet when Betty felt her presence and

turned to face Aunt Zanna, she didn't look wistful or heartbroken. Quite the contrary, she looked a little disgusted. "I'm gonna have to teach Todd how to make a snowball. His always fly apart in midair. You got to pack 'em!" She socked one hand into the palm of the other. "*Pack* 'em!"

For a moment, she was her old self, fierce and vigorous.

Then she took a step toward Zanna and once again she was in the midst of that constant war with gravity, keeping precarious balance as she perched on those unreliable legs.

That's when Zanna realized: She's still the same child. Whatever it was that sent her climbing trees and treating death with such despite, it wasn't killed by the polio, it's still in her as much as ever. It isn't really courage—courage is overcoming fear, and she never felt any. It's more like determination. Not *grim* determination, just a kind of headlong rush toward life, and if her feet couldn't keep up, that wouldn't stop her heart or her mind.

That's why Zanna went ahead and finished the painting.

10

$\mathcal{Z}$anna had taken a Polaroid, once, of Betty walking along the top of a picket fence—an incredible balancing act, actually, but she was so good at it that she was still going even after Zanna rushed into the house to get the camera. And then, just as Zanna was about to snap the picture, a neighbor boy taunted Betty from what he thought was a safe refuge in his yard, two doors down.

Incredibly, Betty reached into her pocket, pulled out a stone—and not a small one—and

from the top of the fence, with the best pitching form, hurled that rock at a speed only
slightly less than David's must have had when
it killed Goliath.

Oh, the wailing from that boy, hit square
in the chest with a stone by a nine-year-old girl.

And Betty's fury at herself—as she lay
sprawled in the petunias—for having missed.
"I was aiming at his big fat mouth!" she insisted as her mother dragged her inside amid a
flurry of Come with me young lady I will not
have you throwing rocks and trying to *kill*
other children even if they deserve it.

Zanna didn't bother following her inside.
She was busy with the Polaroid, waiting all a-
tremble to see the exact moment that the
camera—which wasn't all that good at action
shots—might have captured.

It could not have been better. The photo
had caught her at the exact moment when the
stone released from her hand. And Zanna had
been in exactly the right place to get Betty's
profile—the curl of her lip, the fire in her eyes.
Of course, the fire, now, that wasn't exactly in
the picture. But it would be in the painting!

Zanna had worked on that painting,

whenever she could, what with the morning sickness—much worse than with the first two—and then, after Colleen was born, the endless feedings and the perpetual exhaustion.

She had already captured Betty's face on the canvas, along with the yard and the street and Betty's mother and grandmother—Zanna always roughed in the background first, painting inward toward the heart of the piece— when she got the call from Mother, telling her that little Betty had polio, and could Bug bring the older children to her, since she lived closest of all the family right then?

Zanna put the painting away almost that moment, faced it to the wall, stacked other canvases in front of it. She had a vague idea that if Betty died, then she would finish the painting, so that Bug and Sylvia would have it to remember their marvelous daughter.

Then, when it was clear that Betty would live, but might never walk again, Zanna realized that this painting would be the cruelest thing she could give them. A constant reminder of what they had lost inside that iron lung. Better for them to love and rejoice in the child who eventually escaped that dire machine, and let the other be a distant memory.

What she hadn't understood was Betty herself. The child whose face Zanna had put onto the canvas was still there. That rock was not flung by an arm, it was flung by a *person*. The painting was not a reminder of what was lost, it was the perfect image of something that was very much alive in that girl.

So she went home from that Christmas visit to her parents' house and, despite the fact that Patty was at the "why" age, Lyle was proving that age three can be more terrible than two, and Colleen thought that it was great sport to clamp down on Mama's nipple as hard as she could (this was one child that would not be allowed to continue nursing once the first tooth appeared), Zanna found time to finish that painting of Betty before the first of February.

And then did nothing with it.

What could she do with it? Whom could she show it to, besides Hal? She knew it was perfect—it *was* Betty. The Polaroid had captured the physical shape of the moment, but the soul of the girl in the painting and the love of the mother looking on came from Zanna's love and admiration for the child and from her artist's eye and from her own experience of new motherhood and, yes, from her memory of a lost brother and of a sister she had only seen in dreams.

But just because a painting is perfect does not necessarily mean that it is right to afflict others with the burden of so much emotional freight. If this were a ship, she thought, it would sink under the weight of all that I've stowed below.

So, finished now, the canvas was once again placed against the wall. Hal asked about it only once, sometime during the summer, as they contemplated going to the family picnic back at Mom's and Dad's. "You going to take that painting?"

And it honestly didn't occur to Zanna for a long moment what painting he meant.

"I mean, Sylvia writes that she and Bug are coming and I just wondered."

"No," said Zanna. "They've got a little girl in leg braces. I don't think they want a reminder of how she used to be."

"Your call," he said.

"You think I'm wrong?"

"I think it's your call. Your brother, your painting."

"What do *you* think of it?"

"I think it's your second best painting so far, but I'm no judge of art, you know that."

"Second best?"

His eyes suddenly sparkled from getting a little teary. "Your portrait of you and Ernie will always be my favorite," he said. "Though your technique wasn't yet as strong as it is now." He smiled.

"You sentimental fool, you'll never be an art critic."

"And I know you always wanted to be married to one."

"Is it really a good painting, Hal?"

"It's her to the life. When a painting like that is possible, it just makes me sad for all the people paying so much attention to splashes of paint or geometric figures on canvas."

"So you *are* an art critic."

"I'm saying that even if I didn't already know and love Betty, I would from your painting."

"So maybe someday it'll be seen. But not this year."

11

Zanna was right. Not that year. And not the next. They changed apartments when Colleen needed a bed of her own. And then, after a few more years and Bonnie was born, it was time to pack up and move for real, not just across town. They were joining the vast American pilgrimage to the Next Great Job.

Zanna hadn't looked at the painting in years. When they moved to this apartment she had put it in the back of a stack of canvases that she knew would never be seen, not in this age of modern art, and then she'd gotten busy with momming her way through Patty's first year of school and Lyle's habit of catching the worst case of every childhood disease and Colleen's belief that a silent house was perfect for testing her screaming ability every night.

So when Bug came over to help them box things up for the move—as much to mourn for the fact that he'd be the only one of his family in California now, as to help—Zanna didn't think to steer him away from the painting of Betty pitching that stone.

When she realized that he'd been gone from the living room—or "Boxing Central," as Hal had dubbed it—for a very long time, she got up to go looking for him, and found him in her "studio," sitting in front of a painting, his cheeks streaked with tears. He wasn't even looking at the painting any more. Just looking nowhere, staring into himself, or into the past.

Then she knew at once which painting he was looking at, and she was stricken with remorse.

"Oh, Bug, I never meant you to see that."

He shook his head and held up a hand to stop her.

She came over and took his hand and sank down beside him and put her head on his shoulder. "I took a Polaroid of that moment," she said. "I had to finish it because . . ."

"Because it's Betty," said Bug.

"Is it? It's certainly the way I see her."

Bug nodded. "She's still like that, you know."

"I do know. I finished it after she was in leg braces, Bug. Because I saw she still had that . . ."

"Fire," said Bug.

"But I never meant to make you face her that way, before the polio."

"Are you kidding?" He looked at her in wonderment. "No, of course—you didn't want to bring back—but don't you see? We thought we were the only ones who still saw this Betty. The girl behind the leg armor. Can I show it to Sylvia?"

"Are you sure she'll feel the way you do?"

"She'll feel the way *she* does, whatever that is, but she should know this painting exists."

"If you want it, Bug, it's yours. It was always for you."

He started sobbing and turned and held on to her.

"I take it that's a yes?" she said.

He nodded into her shoulder.

Later, when the painting was wrapped in brown paper for the long drive back home, Bug rested his hand on it and said, "She's not beat yet, you know. She moves around the house without the braces as much as she can—leaning on walls and furniture and whoever's nearby, but without the metal on her legs. She'll never run, but she'll walk. And she can't throw a fastball like a big leaguer any more, but whatever she throws hits what she was aiming at."

"I'm glad to hear that."

"I'm just saying that she won't be beat. That's why this is still a portrait of our little girl as she *is*, and not just as she was."

Then he shook hands with Hal (because that was after men forgot how to hug each other and before they remembered again) and gave a kiss to Zanna, and then he was gone.

So were they, a few days later, the moving

truck taking all their worldly possessions, including her paintings, across the country, while Hal and Zanna took turns driving a '56 Buick full of squirming poking whining laughing singing children along the two-lane highways that linked the cities of America, a frail web dotted with Burma Shave signs and one-pump gas stations and motor courts that you inspected for fleas before you paid the night's rent. It was a glorious trip that the older children never forgot. The kind of trip that in later years would make Zanna turn to Hal and say, "Wouldn't you like to pile the kids into the car and go somewhere?"

To which Hal would say, "Why not just put the iron on high and press my head? That'll be much cheaper and faster." But he knew what she meant, and hugged her for the memory.

Bug didn't make it back home for the next summer's reunion, or Christmas either. And the next few reunions were darkened by Todd's accusations against Patty and Lyle, and then by Zanna's accusation against Todd, so the subject of Betty's painting didn't come up.

Betty was there herself, anyway, so who needed the painting? No one saw leg braces by then. In fact, Hal once speculated that Bug had stayed away from family gatherings for that year or so because Betty didn't want to go until she had the braces off for good.

She was vivacious and full of talk, and she happily tended the littlest kids while the older, more athletic ones took off on adventures she could no longer keep up with. But she was sturdy enough on her legs to chase after toddlers who were trying to make their getaway, and she had a gentle hand with the little ones.

Zanna wondered sometimes about her painting of Betty—wondered mostly if Betty herself had ever seen it, and if she remembered being that girl. But then, she couldn't *wish* for Betty to see it, because despite her cheerfulness, it was impossible to know what grief the girl might still suffer, hidden from all eyes except, perhaps, those fierce eyes in the painting.

Then came the invitation to Betty's wedding. She was nineteen, which was older than many girls, but still young enough to suggest that her physical frailty, those impossibly skinny legs, had not been much of an obstacle to her finding a boy who'd value her. And to Zanna's delight, Betty had asked to have her wedding in the same church where her parents had gotten married.

Which meant that the big family picnic was held in June that year instead of August, for this was the first wedding in the generation and, except for Davy's oldest, who was clerking for a state supreme court justice and couldn't get away, they were all there.

Zanna was the last one into the chapel, it seemed—so many last-minute things to attend to, getting her own kids ready and respectable—and Hal already had them inside before she was done with her last primping in the rear-view mirror and came up the steps into the church.

There in the foyer, on an easel behind the guest book, was her painting of Betty, in an ornate wooden frame with a small brass plaque engraved with the title: "Betty Silencing the Neighbor Boy."

It was just about the last thing Zanna expected to see.

"I think this painting constitutes fair warning to the bridegroom, about what he's getting into, don't you think?" Hal's arm slipped around her shoulders.

"You're supposed to be sitting on the kids to keep them quiet."

"Let 'em scream," said Hal. "Hollering children—that's the proper prelude to a marriage, not that stupid wedding march."

"I can't believe they used this painting," said Zanna. "The portrait of the bride is supposed to be a beautiful color photo in her wedding dress with a blurred background. Like a goddess."

"Oh, this is a goddess all right," said Hal. "Or at least one of the Furies."

And then, completely to her own surprise, Zanna turned to her husband and clutched his lapels and pressed her face into his tie and tried very, very hard not to cry.

"You're getting face powder on my tie."

"The only makeup I wear is lipstick," said Zanna. "But I'll kiss your tie if you want something to complain about."

"Are you kidding? I could hold you like this all day. Let 'em bury us in rice."

"We really should go in," said Zanna.

"You first."

She pushed against him even harder, and he held her tighter, and then at the same moment they each let go. She was smiling now. "They liked the painting," she said.

"More to the point," said Hal, "*Betty* likes the painting."

"You think so?"

"Nothing is displayed at the wedding without the bride's consent, or she might stamp her pretty little foot and the world will end."

"I wonder what the groom thinks of it."

"From the look in Betty's eye, I'd say he should keep his objections, should he have any, to himself."

At that moment, Bug and Betty rushed into the foyer from one of the waiting rooms, with several local women herding the flower girls and the ring-bearer, who were the most solemn people. Not one of them spared even a glance at Hal and Zanna, standing near the door. Zanna looked from the woman holding her father's arm to the girl in the painting and, yes, even at that age, Betty had already been the woman she would grow up to be; and even after polio, Betty was still the girl she had been back then.

"They already knew," whispered Zanna.

"Who knew what?" asked Hal.

"My parents—they already knew the man that Ernie would grow up to be. Because they knew the boy." Then she glanced at the painting and Hal nodded.

The signal was given from the door, the wedding march started, and the parade began, with Hal and Zanna watching from behind.

When the bride and her father had gone, Hal stepped forward and caught the door. For a moment he and Zanna waited, watching Betty and Bug go up the aisle. You had to be watching for it to know Betty had a limp. Though of course, Zanna realized, that very thought meant that she *had* been watching for it.

"I just had a terrible thought," whispered Hal. "If kids don't change when they grow up, what about Todd?"

"Todd's turned into a human," said Zanna. "That was just a phase."

"I've read *Wind in the Willows*. I know all about Mr. Toad."

"Todd will turn out all right. He's Bug's son, isn't he? And my nephew."

"Make sure you tell that to the judge at the sentencing hearing."

"You're evil, Hal," said Zanna. "Now let's make our humiliating dash up the aisle and see if we can get into our seats before anybody says 'I do.'"

The wedding was lovely—none of that hippie nonsense about saying made-up vows and reciting bad poetry. If Betty had been that kind of young woman, she would never have brought this party to her grandparents' church.

After the ceremony, by the time Hal and Zanna had suffered through all the teasing about their late arrival, the painting had been removed from the foyer so it wouldn't get knocked over, and they didn't see it again that day. Betty's new husband was an athlete, by the look of him, and after she threw the bouquet, he scooped her up, dress and all, and *ran* down the church steps, with Sylvia screaming, "Don't drop my baby!" while everybody else laughed and cheered and threw rice. Then he set her, gentle as a rose petal, into the passenger seat of the convertible they had borrowed for the occasion, and with a few happy tootles on the car horn, they were off.

The picnic was the next day. It was just like always, except Sylvia was a little teary-eyed during the cutting of the cake, and Bug looked a little dazed.

Then there came the time, into the summer evening, as the sun was nearing the horizon, when everything was packed up and loaded into cars and the families began the drive from the park to the folks' place, as Grandma's and Grandpa's old house was called. Only, again without a word being said, the cars all took a side trip to a cemetery where they parked, and most of the adults began the quiet walk to the well-known gravesite.

Mother almost never cried during these visits, so it was a real surprise when she burst into tears this evening. It only lasted a moment, but she seemed to feel she owed an explanation. "I'm sorry," she said. "I just couldn't help thinking how much I wish I could have seen Ernie walk up that aisle. And then wonder what *his* children would have looked like. Really, I know it's silly of me, and now I've spoiled everybody's day and . . ."

Father silenced her with an arm across her shoulder. "Nobody minds. We were all thinking the same thing. It doesn't spoil anything, to miss the ones who aren't here."

Zanna had been thinking the same thing, only about her twin, and remembering that there were things her twin got to do that *she* had missed out on. So maybe it all came out even in the end.

She couldn't say that to anyone, though. She just held Hal's hand and smiled at her mother when she looked her way.

It was Sylvia who made Mother feel better about having cried. "I know it's not the same thing, Mom," she said. "But there was somebody else missing at today's wedding."

Everyone waited for her to say who.

"We had her portrait on an easel in the foyer."

Mother and Davy and Lucy all started to protest, but Bug silenced them with a gesture. "We know Betty's the same girl," he said. "We know that. But she led a different life. She had a different childhood. That's all Sylvia meant."

Then Sylvia, tears in her eyes, walked over to Zanna and clasped her hands. "That picture has meant so much to us, I hope you know that. And it was Betty who insisted on showing it. We meant to keep it private, but she said you wouldn't mind. She said, After all, I was standing on top of a picket fence in the front yard when I threw that stone. I *meant* to be seen by everybody!"

They had a laugh at that.

And then Davy said, "It's not the same thing as losing a child outright, like you did, Mom and Dad. Or having a child go through such suffering as Betty did. But Lucy and I were saying to each other, how much we miss the little ones, now that they're growing up. Every stage of their lives, from scraping poop off their butts to putting Band-Aids on their knees, it goes by so fast, and you can't hold onto it, it's just there and gone. And just because you miss the child that's gone doesn't mean you don't love the woman or man that's still with you."

There was a long moment of silence after that. Then Father said, "Well, I've had about all the wisdom I can take for one day. Who wants to go back home with me?"

He led the parade of children back toward the cars, and Lucy and Sylvia and Hall soon took over the shepherding, and in a few moments Father slipped back, and there they were, just the five of them who had known Ernie, gathered around his grave and the grave of the baby sister that only Ernie, of all of them, had ever had a chance to know.

There came a time like this at every family gathering—in a hot summer evening after the picnic, or on a crisp Christmas night, when Davy, Bug, and Zanna gathered with their parents at Ernie's and Dianna's graves.

Sometimes they spoke cheerfully of their memories of Ernie, and of each other as children, all their past brought together into the present moment, being there with the people who had been with them then.

Sometimes they said little.

Sometimes, like this time, Mother wept.

And one time, years later, when he was very old and had been brought to the gravesides in his wheelchair, Father wept too.

"It never fades," he explained. "You don't think of them as often, but when you do, it's like an old injury that aches when the weather turns."

They murmured their understanding, and it was true, they *did* understand. Not because their own feelings for Ernie were as sharp as their parents' feelings, but because they had children of their own, and they knew.

Father added, as they wheeled him away from the graves: "Won't have to miss him much longer."

And he didn't. The next family gathering was only a few months later, and this time there were three graves. Mother had arranged for Father's tombstone to include her name and date of birth and even the dash before the space where her death would be recorded.

"But Mother," said Bug. "It's morbid. As if you're just waiting to die."

"I *am*," she said irritably. "You think I can't read a calendar?"

"Well, don't be in a hurry about it," said Davy, putting an arm around her.

"I can be in a hurry if I want to," she said. "Oh, your father can wait—he spent half his life jangling the car keys, waiting for me, so he's used to it. And Ernie—you think I don't know he's been busy, wherever he is? That wasn't a boy to sit still. But that girl Dianna. I don't even *know* her. Did you think of that? I don't even know her, and I've waited a long enough time, I should think!"

But she had eleven more years to wait— long enough to see all three of her children become grandparents in their own right, and to have pictures taken of her holding each of five different great-grandchildren, along with the baby's parents and grandparents. She loved the pictures. "There it is, right in that snapshot—a whole genealogy, a family tree! And I'm the root. Don't you forget that!"

Then she, too, was laid in the grave that waited for her. The family plot was complete now; when it came the others' time to die, they would be in their own family plots some-where. Only the children who died without families of their own needed to lie where their parents lay.

The family reunions ended then. Without the folks' place to gather at, there seemed lit-tle point in it. But from time to time, when they had a reason to be near, Davy, Bug, or Zanna would take a side trip to that cemetery in the town of their childhood, and lay flowers on the graves, and speak to beloved parents and long-lost siblings.

What they didn't realize, but would have been very glad to know, was how many of their own children also found at least one chance, in their comings and goings through the world, to visit those graves, and lay flowers there. For even though they had never met these children whose names were now so weathered on the stones, they had been part of their lives all the same, part of what it meant to be a family, part of their understand-ing of that vague and difficult word *love*.

12

$\mathcal{S}$uzanna Pullman was in her sixties when, to her great surprise, she became famous, in a smallish way. She had never painted as a career, because by the time she got to college, it was clear that the only way to get the approval of the art faculty was to paint things that nobody could understand.

And if there was one thing Zanna was determined never to do, it was to paint something that would prompt someone to ask, "What *is* it?"

So, ignoring the orthodoxy

of the painting world, she created landscapes and portraits and still lifes and the kind of romantic art that she had come to love. She liked to tell people that she had learned painting from dead forgotten artists, and when they pressed her for a list, she would list her mentors: Chase, Bouguereau, Alma-Tadema, Leighton, Poynter. People would look at her blankly.

But she placed some of her canvases in a local gallery, and they all sold, sometimes within days, sometimes after a year or so, but someone would value her work and ask about her. And the money came in handy—they liked to say that Mom's art put all her kids through college, though sometimes Hal would say that he'd rather have used the money to put in a pool.

Then, in her old age, the fashion suddenly changed and her list of mentors was on everyone's lips and serious collectors began to take notice of paintings by Suzanna Pullman. The gallery put another zero on the end of their asking price.

People bought her work all the more quickly.

There was a write-up in an art magazine, and an interview on NPR, and then a piece of hers on the cover of *Time*. (But not her face—she absolutely insisted that her face had nothing to say, it was all in her art, and refused to let them point a camera at her no matter what excuse they fed her.)

There was money, then, and her grandchildren were surprised to find that Grandma was cool. She only wished her Hal had lived to see it; but he had been carried off by a cold that turned into pneumonia so quickly that he died in the emergency room, gasping for air. She grieved for him but also thought: So much better to go that way than to linger with some painful disease, or with Alzheimer's, or crippled by age. Good old pneumonia. But of course that was self-deception, except that she wasn't even fooled. She missed him every day.

Then it all settled down again and life was normal and Granny Zan was still Granny Zan, a tough-minded old lady who was always happy to have a visit as long as you didn't make a sound outside her studio door between six and eleven A.M. "I have to make hay while the light is right," she'd say.

Only a few of her grandchildren had any particular interest in the arts, and most of them were performers, some with music, one on stage. There was a boy who dabbled in sculpture. A girl who tried her hand at watercolors but lost interest when it was clear that she wouldn't instantly become as famous as Granny Zan.

The arty ones weren't her favorites anyway—they always seemed either self-centered or overly competitive and she found both attitudes boring.

Her favorites were the grandchildren who would spend the afternoon in the kitchen with her, baking. "Talk about lost arts," she'd say. "My mother baked bread or *something* almost every day. I grew up surrounded by cookies and cake and homemade bread and biscuits and panfried scones, and no packaged mix ever crossed my mother's threshold. I'd be ashamed to see the Pillsbury Doughboy's squishy little butt inside my pantry, and as for Betty Crocker, she's such a *gossip* and she has been known to use powdered eggs in her cakes."

It was one of those favored grandchildren who stopped by her house at Christmastime, planning to make it just a quick visit as she drove on to her boyfriend's parents' house in another state in time for Christmas Eve. It was only coincidence that her name was Diana— she was named for her mother's mother, and not for Zanna's twin, as the missing *n* attested. She was clearly in love with the boy who had driven her here, a half-shaven starved-looking boy named Jake, which to Zanna sounded like what you'd call an outhouse when she was a girl. But he was kind and attentive to Diana, and for that reason Zanna gave him the bene-fit of the doubt.

She showed them through the house and then let them sample the cookies she was bak-ing for the neighbors. "I tried making my mother's date bread, but nobody knew what to do with them. Exotic baked fruits just can't compete with Chee-tos and Fritos and Doritos and Tostitos, I guess. And I can see from your faces that you are both *oh* so grateful that you didn't happen to come by on a date bread day, but you needn't worry, I don't force my treats on anybody, any more than I make anybody take my paintings who doesn't want them."

They answered her by rhapsodizing over the perfection of her cookies and they had spent the whole afternoon together before anyone looked out the window and realized that it was snowing heavily.

"Well, I don't like that," said Zanna. "Not a bit."

"We'd better get going," said Jake. "There's a mountain range between us and home and it gets nasty in a storm."

"Indeed it does," said Zanna, "and now I want to ask you, Jake, which would your mother rather have? A living son who is a day late getting home for Christmas, or a dead son who proved his love by trying to go over the pass at night, in a snowstorm?"

Zanna held up a hand to silence her granddaughter. "I already know what *your* mother would prefer," said Zanna, "and that you won't pay the slightest attention to me once your mind is made up. But Jake here is much more sensible than you are—and he loves his mother more than you love yours, so you don't even get a vote here. Well, Jake, what is it? Over the mountain, hurrying home, and your mother spends all the remaining Christmases of her life weeping over a grave? Or do the two of you stay here, have Christmas morning with me, and then go over the pass after the snow has stopped and they've had a chance to plow the roads?"

Jake looked at Diana, who was shaking her head grimly—determined to go on, of course, being the girl she was.

"I'm not going to pretend here," said Zanna. "I'm old-fashioned and you two aren't married, so if you stay with me it'll be separate rooms."

Diana blushed and Jake protested. "We aren't sleeping together."

"Not *everybody* does that, you know, Granny Zan!"

"Well, good, so that's one less reason for you to try to get out of my house before Christmas."

129

In the end, they stayed, and Zanna liked the way Jake teased Diana into not being mad about having things not go her way. Yes, this boy could marry Diana without having her run him around on the end of a stick, and that meant they'd both have a chance for happiness. Don't let go of this one, you stubborn girl. Even if he doesn't have the tiniest shred of a hope of a career, at least so far.

Zanna was untroubled by the fact that she hadn't bought them anything for Christmas. She dug out some old Christmas stockings and safety-pinned their names to them and hung them beside hers over the fireplace.

"All I ever get is coal," she said, "and after I bullied you into staying here Christmas Eve, it's bound to be anthracite for me again this year."

She left them watching television and went to bed before them. At three A.M., just like clockwork, she woke up with her bladder ready to burst and so thirsty she could hardly swallow. Of all an old woman's bodily functions, why did her kidneys have to get *more* efficient as she got older?

But once she had gone to the bathroom, and then to the kitchen to sip a little cranberry juice, she walked around the house. Being human, she had to check on the children, and was pleased to see that they had not only gone to bed in separate rooms, they had left the doors ajar so she could see for herself.

What she was really doing, though, was searching for gifts to put in their stockings. She was old enough that she had accumulated a lifetime's worth of possessions, and now it was time to start parting with some of them, when the right person came along. Indeed, long before he died, she and Hal had started giving nothing but food as gifts. "No reason to clutter up people's houses with things they can't get rid of for fear you'll come to visit and notice they didn't keep it," they said to anyone who asked. People got the idea, and stopped giving *them* things—though few were brave enough to bake for them, and so what they got were bookstore gift certificates or donations to some cause in their name.

Still, that didn't mean she didn't have a house full of knickknacks in true grandma fashion—it just guaranteed that all of them were old.

For Jake, she chose a porcelain of a haughty-looking woman in a Marie-Antoinette dress, all lace and very intricately painted. She would tell him it was to remind him that when a woman got too proud, there was always someone ready to cut off her head.

And for Diana, she took her ancient copy of *The Bobbsey Twins of Lakeport* and inscribed it, "This book was at the heart of my childhood. Keep it for a child of yours someday, and if you don't have one, then read it yourself and think of Granny Zan."

Then she filled several plastic sandwich bags with cookies and biscuits for the road, and of course a couple of apples because that had been an inevitable part of Christmas stockings when she was a girl.

When she came into the living room to fill their stockings, she was surprised to see that there was something in her own—and when she felt through the sock, she could tell it wasn't coal after all.

Well, of course, they wouldn't have come

empty-handed to visit her, so when they had to stay over on Christmas Eve, they decided to slip it into her stocking. It felt like a book, and that would be nice, a book was like food, you could consume it and pass it along. She'd open it tomorrow. She was a big girl now. She could wait to find out what Santa had brought.

Then she got out an old crayon picture in a frame and set it on the mantel. "Not long now, Ernie," she said. "If you still remember who I am."

In the morning, she was awakened by their whispering and pan-banging in the kitchen. Just like we used to wake Mom and Dad by our noisy efforts to be quiet, she thought.

Sure enough, Diana had been bold enough to try to make flapjacks in Granny Zan's kitchen—and to Zanna's pleasant surprise, they were very good. They had a wonderful time over breakfast, chatting about Jake's family and his memories of Christmas and how all three of them had grown up in families with completely different Christmas traditions.

"But everybody has stockings," said Zanna,

and they agreed. Which was the cue to go into the living room.

They were delighted to see that their stockings were stuffed so full they had had to be removed from the mantel and laid on the couch, and of course Jake thanked her and Diana teasingly cursed her for supplying them with enough calories to relieve a famine. Only when they got to the bottom of the stockings and found their real presents did they get serious.

"This is a family heirloom," said Jake, but Zanna answered him with the speech she had prepared, which made him laugh and Diana growl until she laughed, and Jake said, "I'll keep this, then, to remember what it's like to love a proud woman."

When Diana read the inscription inside *The Bobbsey Twins*, though, a couple of tears spilled down her cheeks. "Uncle Bug told me once that he used to read this to you when you were little. He didn't think this copy still existed."

"Still does," said Zanna. "I hope it always will—but that it will be used, too."

"It will," said Diana, saying it like the most solemn of covenants.

Then Jake reached down under the tree and picked up a brightly wrapped box and handed it to her. "Diana didn't know what we could bring you," he said, "because you have everything and besides, you can't buy art for Picasso, so we couldn't get you anything edible *or* decorative."

Zanna took the wrapping paper off meticulously, a habit she had begun in order to annoy her brothers during the present-opening ceremony, but which now she did because it simply felt like the right way to open a gift.

Inside it was a CD, but one with no cover and nothing written on it. "We recorded it ourselves," explained Jake. "On the computer. You do have a CD player, don't you?"

"I know all about CDs, and about ripping songs off the internet," said Granny Zan. "You aren't going to go to federal prison for making this for me, are you?"

"We didn't *rip* it," said Diana. "It's us. Singing. We sang every Christmas carol we know. We're not very good, but then if you picture us standing out in the snow shivering while we sing it, your standards will get lower and you'll like it better."

She hugged them both. "I will listen to it a dozen times today."

"No you won't," said Jake.

"We have a bet that you can't even get through it once," said Diana. "We're not professionals. We shouldn't have tried this at home."

"I *am* a musician," said Jake, "but not a singer."

"And I'm not a musician of any kind," said Diana.

By this point, Zanna was at her stocking, feeling where there had been a present in it last night. There was nothing there.

"Sorry," said Jake. "We didn't think of filling your stocking. The CD might have fit, if I'd thought about it."

Zanna looked at Diana, who blushed.

"Second thoughts?" asked Zanna.

Diana nodded.

"Any chance of third thoughts?"

Diana reached into her purse and took out a slim book and handed it to Zanna.

Jake was impressed. "Man, you put *that* in her stocking?"

"What I am," said Diana, "is a very bad poet with delusions of grandeur."

"What she is," said Jake, "is the greatest living American poet, and she still won't let me set any of her poems to music. My goal is to someday be good enough that she'll let me."

"But if this is the book where you keep your poems," said Zanna.

"No," said Diana. "It's a copy. I copied them out for you, so you could read it."

"And I bet you left out the really sexy ones."

Diana gasped and Jake laughed and Zanna was delighted that she had struck home. Meanwhile, she had the book open and was thumbing through, looking at the titles.

"I like to think I write poems the way you paint," said Diana. "Clearly. So people can understand what I'm talking about."

And then Zanna came to a certain page and stopped. The title of the poem was, "Zanna's Gift for Ernie."

"Father told me about the drawing that

you always had out for every Christmas," said Diana. "He always said that you told him it was a drawing that a little girl once made for her brother as a Christmas present. I got Uncle Bug to tell me the whole story last summer."

Diana walked to the mantel. "Is this it? The original?"

"Yes," said Zanna. "Not much sign of talent in it, is there?" Then she looked back down at the poem and resumed reading while Diana and Jake studied the picture.

When they turned to face each other again, both Zanna and Diana had tears in their eyes. "Oh, my darling," said Zanna, "how could you understand this, when you've never had any children of your own?"

"I *was* a child," Diana answered. "And I have an imagination. And besides, I've known *you* my whole life. As Uncle Bug says, you haven't changed a bit since you were little."

"Well, you have just given me the best present I can remember," said Zanna. "I'm so proud of you." She looked at her proudly. "Just think. You're kin of mine!"

"Well that's how I feel about *you*," said

Diana, and they hugged and laughed. "I thought that maybe you'd like them. But I almost didn't include that one poem, because it was so presumptuous of me."

Zanna assured her that it wasn't a *bit* presumptuous, and then, to Diana's embarrassment, she read the poem aloud. It was the story of the little girl who had a present for her brother but no way to give it to him. The language was simple, the rhyming subtle, the flow of it like music.

"You see why I want to set it to music," said Jake. "But then, music would be redundant, wouldn't it?"

"Diana, you really need to marry a man who knows how to flatter you like that. I married one who let me continue my very time-consuming hobby during all the years when nobody wanted to hear about the kind of painting that I did. But you, I don't think you'll have to wait so long for the world to see your talent. And then all kinds of rock stars and movie actors will want to marry you, and I can promise you, this Jake fellow is better than any of *them*."

It was nice to see that Jake could blush.

By noon they were on their way, a phone call to the highway patrol having ascertained that the pass was indeed clear and traffic was unobstructed. They ate cookies and biscuits all the way to Jake's mother's house, where the family—including three teenage siblings—had waited Christmas for them.

And as they drove that long road, Zanna, baking again in her kitchen, listened to their CD four times over, singing along on most of the songs.

13

Three years later, late in November, just a few days after Thanksgiving, Diana and Jake received a package at their apartment in Milwaukee. The return address said it was from Suzanna Pullman.

"But that's impossible," said Diana.

"She must have mailed it before she died," said Jake.

Granny Zan had passed away only a few days before. They would have gone to the funeral, but they couldn't afford the flight, and Diana was too pregnant to risk flying anyway.

Even as Diana was opening the package, she knew what it was. "It's Zanny's gift to Ernie," she whispered, and so it was, once the paper was off: a simple frame holding a meticulously drawn and completely unintelligible child's drawing.

There was a note. "I have it memorized," Granny Zan had written in her spidery hand. "And I have a feeling I'm only a day or two away from being able to give Ernie the version in my memory. So I have no more use for the physical version of it. There'd be no shortage of art collectors who'd fight over Suzanna Pullman's earliest surviving work. But I wanted it to go to someone who loved what it meant, without thinking about what it would go for. You showed me that you understood a child's heart, even if you couldn't understand a child's painting. So this is for you from little Zanna Pullman. It was you I was saving it for all these years, after all.

Love, Granny Zan."

Jake leaned over Diana's shoulder and

kissed her on the cheek. "Such a reunion they're having."

"Oh, I hope so," said Diana. "After they waited so long, God wouldn't disappoint them now."

"She had twice the life most people have," said Jake.

"Well, of course," said Diana. "She was living for two."

Later, sitting on the couch, looking up at Zanna's gift sitting on the mantel, Jake put his hand on Diana's abdomen and said, "I don't think he'd appreciate it if we named him Zanna."

"There'll be girls later," said Diana, "and the name Suzanna will certainly belong to one of them."

"But this boy?"

"Ernest isn't a regular name anymore," said Diana. "But maybe as a middle name?"

And that's the name they gave him, meaning to call him Jacob, his first name. But long before he was old enough to learn his own name, they had fallen into the habit of calling him Ernie all the time. By the time he was three, there was indeed a little Zanna ready to grow up just behind him.

And every Christmas, their parents brought out a child's drawing in a cheap little frame, waiting eagerly to tell their children what it meant, and whom they were named for, and how grief is just another name for love.